Francesca Sanna

ME AND MY MY FEAR

Flying Eye Books
London | New York

I have always had a secret.
A tiny friend called Fear.

Fear has always looked after me and kept me safe.

Together we have explored new
things and stuck by each other.

But since we came to this new country,
Fear isn't so little anymore.

She keeps growing and growing.

I want to go outside and discover my new neighbourhood...

...but Fear won't move.

And when I have to go to school,
Fear doesn't want me to go.

Fear hates my new school. When the teacher says my name wrong, she grows angry...

...even though I know it was just an accident.

At break time, Fear keeps me all to herself.

I don't understand anyone
and they don't understand me.

When school is over, Fear can't wait to go home.

And at dinner, Fear eats all the food she can.

At night, in my new room, Fear dreams
so loudly that I can't sleep.

I feel more and more
lonely every day.

Fear says it's because
no one likes me.

Well, I don't like it here!

But what's this? A boy in my class
wants to show me something.

Soon we begin to draw and paint together.

At break time, I want to go outside and play with the boy.

As we run through the playground,
suddenly a dog barks at us through the fence.

"**AARRGH**!" the boy screams and hides quickly behind something strange and small.

He has a secret fear like me!

I thought **I** was the only one to have one.

Fear is getting smaller each day.
And school is not so difficult anymore.

It's still not easy to understand everything,
but I've started to notice that everyone else has a fear, too...

...and sometimes we all play together!

AUTHOR'S NOTE

I am a very anxious person, and at times when working on this book my fear would grow too big, and grip me too tightly. I would not have succeeded without the precious help of many people. Firstly, I would like to thank each and every child I met in schools and libraries, who was willing to share their fears about being the new one, the different one, the one from another country. They helped keep my own fear from growing too large.

I am also immensely grateful for the support and precious insights of Dr Jessica Reinisch and everyone on The Reluctant Internationalists project at Birkbeck, University of London, who hosted me and assisted my research for this book. Finally, I would like to thank Harriet, who believed in this project and helped me put together all the pieces.

Endorsed by Amnesty International for reminding us that every child
has the right to express their feelings, relax and play with friends.